LOVE IN THE PAST TENSE

A HAYWARD HALL SHORT STORY

ALEXANDRIA BLAELOCK

BlueMere Books
MELBOURNE, AUSTRALIA

For permission requests, please contact
enquiries@bluemerebooks.com.

Ordering Information:
Discounts are available on quantity purchases. For details, contact orders@bluemerebooks.com.

Love in the Past Tense/Alexandria Blaelock
paperback ISBN: 978-1-925749-56-4
digital ISBN: 978-1-925749-57-1

Book Layout © BookDesignTemplates.com

LOVE IN THE PAST TENSE

With next to no noise, Roberts, his father's valet, eased the bedroom door open and brought in a cup of tea.

"Good morning Young Master Henry." He sat the cup on the bedside table before opening the curtains to let the dull sunlight stream in on the mostly awake Master Fox.

Henry Fox had inherited Hayward Hall when his father died suddenly some six months before, and he, as well as the servants, were having a hard time adjusting to his new station in life.

Surely 28 years old was sufficiently old to not feel like a child dressing up.

He sat up, waved the shamefaced valet away to the dressing room and reached for the tea. Giving it an unnecessary stir with the silver spoon, he took a sip and looked through the large windows, out over the formal gardens. Partially obscured by the rain.

They were nice enough, though a little old fashioned; he'd have to do something about that at some point.

But he missed his father enough to not want to mess with anything just yet, and besides, he knew it would upset his mother. After all, the garden was an act of love for her.

She walked the paths every day. Often with Miss Viola Seagrove in attendance.

What he could do though, was get rid of some of this monstrous mahogany furniture and oppressively dark, striped wallpaper.

Or perhaps it could wait until he married. To the ubiquitous Miss Seagrove

Who would no doubt have an Opinion about what should replace it.

He sighed.

Conveniently she was staying at the house, ostensibly as a companion to his mother, but presumably, their goal was to ensure she became his wife.

His mother adored her, and he didn't actively dislike her, so he'd been prepared to go with the flow for his mother's sake.

It wasn't as if they would be joined at the hip forever after.

He sighed once more, drank the rest of his tea, then heaved himself out of the bed, and into the day.

As he took care of his ablutions in the bathroom, he blessed his father's foresight for including plumbed in bathrooms in the house design. Controversial at the time, but damned convenient now.

Moving into the Master bedroom had been worth it just for the attached bath and dressing rooms. Not to mention not having to share with his brothers.

Roberts, presented a fashionable black pinstriped wool morning suit, with a contrasting blue patterned vest. Paired with a white Arundel collar shirt, black silk bow tie, and the peacock feather patterned braces embroidered by his mother.

In a small act of rebellion, he chose the brown oxfords instead of black.

Roberts smoothed the suit over his shoulders and brushed it out while Henry threaded the bar of his father's watch through his waistcoat.

Watch in his right waistcoat pocket, penknife in his left, and adjusted the fall of the locket fob.

He flicked open the locket to see the photograph of his mother on the left, and himself as a baby on the right. It was something he'd seen his father do countless times when faced with a big decision.

He'd hoped one day to replace his photograph with his wife's, but couldn't quite imagine Miss Seagrove's face in place, smiling slightly back at him like his mother.

He snapped the locket shut, grimaced at himself in the mirror for a moment and smoothed the hair on his head and moustache once last time.

Ideally, he'd like the kind of love match his parents had shared. But he couldn't imagine sharing that intense closeness with anyone. Not anyone he knew, and certainly not Miss "call me Viola" Seagrove.

Turning away, before straightening his shoulders and leaving to do battle in the dining room.

He could get breakfast in his room but didn't want to trouble the servants. They had enough dealing with his mother.

The dining room was also full of monstrous mahogany furniture, though the vine patterned wallpaper was less oppressive.

As the house was still in mourning, the extra chairs and dining table leaves were packed away leaving a more intimate setting for just the family.

"Good Morning," he said as he entered the room.

Four of his brothers were arguing with two of his sisters, and they interrupted their quarrelling for long enough to return his greeting.

His mother was trying unsuccessfully to referee.

Knowing the other three were making Nanny's life hell somewhere else in the house made it almost bearable.

"And how are you this fine morning," Miss Seagrove simpered.

Henry grunted and collected his choice of breakfast items from the buffet. The mahogany buffet.

He rolled his eyes at the wall.

At both the buffet and Miss Seagrove.

She had snagged the seat next to the head of the table, so he had to either sit next to her or demote himself, neither of the options particularly appealing.

He shook out the day's *The Argus* newspaper, September 9th, 1904.

He didn't have to feign interest in an article about the day's solar eclipse while shovelling breakfast into his mouth.

Miss Seagrove didn't take the hint, "you seem a little peaky, have you perhaps been drinking a little too much whisky?"

Henry grunted and raised the newspaper a little so she couldn't see him over it.

Wasn't she perhaps taking somewhat of a liberty with the intimacy afforded by his mother?

He flipped over to the weather, "Freshening northern winds, gradually becoming unsettled."

It was already unsettled here, and he was going to give himself indigestion the speed with which he was eating.

"Would you consider joining your mother and me for a walk in the garden after breakfast?"

He grunted again.

On second thoughts, he wasn't sure he could go with the flow. He was starting to dislike her.

Why did he think he needed to marry her again?

"I'm quite sure it would do you the world of good."

He folded the newspaper, placed his cutlery side by side on his plate, and sculled his tea.

"I really don't think so Miss Seagrove, I must organise my speech notes.

He sketched a quick incline of his shoulders in her direction before she could say *Please, call me Viola*, and almost sprinted from the dining room.

Dammit, he left the newspaper behind.

Back in his room, he looked out the window.

He couldn't go to the library as he'd be fair game for the rest of his family.

And the study held too many memories of his father.

But he didn't really want to spend the day skulking in his bedroom.

He was about to open his pocket watch when a woman threw the door open.

At least he thought it was a woman.

She had short red hair and appeared to be wearing some kind of figure-hugging swimsuit.

She ran across the room and slapped the watch from his hand.

"What the devil do you think you're doing?" he demanded.

"I'm saving you from yourself."

She threw herself in his arms, crashing into his body. He took a step back to stabilise his stance, but distracted by her floral fragrance, couldn't correct sufficiently to prevent them from falling to the floor.

She was incredibly heavy.

And wasn't wearing a corset.

"Er, Miss?"

She didn't respond.

He shook her arm, and she didn't respond.

"Miss?"

Oh, that was just fabulous.

She'd passed out.

He lay on the floor, thinking if he was dreaming, it wasn't such a bad dream. A Bathing Beauty saving him from himself.

Roberts chose that moment to enter the bedroom, then turned to go.

"Wait," Henry said.

Roberts turned his body, but not his face towards his employer.

"Er, yes Mr Fox?"

"You can see her, right?"

"Of course, how could I not see a half-naked woman in your bedroom?"

Henry let out a sigh of relief, "that's excellent, I'm not imagining it. Would you help me get her to the bed?"

Roberts lifted her shoulders, allowing Henry to wriggle out from underneath her, and together they managed to carry her to his bed.

"What now?" Henry asked.

Roberts looked at him, and after a beat, said, "you're the boss."

"Oh, right.

"I suppose we should find somewhere for her to stay. Should it be servants or guests?" Henry looked at the valet.

Roberts didn't say anything.

Henry looked at him some more.

"The Blue Bedroom by the stairs is currently unoccupied, I'll ask one of the maids do it up."

"Good."

Roberts left the room.

Henry dragged a chair over to the bed and watched her.

She was quite pale, with dark shadows under her eyes.

He wondered how she'd got into the house, and up the stairs without anyone raising the alarm.

And for that matter, where had she come from that no one between there and here had batted an eyelid.

That she'd lost her hair suggested hospital - the closest was The Alfred Hospital. Could she have walked for an hour to get here?

Not in that get-up.

Or had she somehow escaped from the Point Nepean Quarantine Station? But that would have taken days, and she seemed too fresh for that.

It was as if she'd bathed just before opening his door.

He wanted to keep her to himself, and not tell anyone, but at the very least she'd need some proper clothes.

If he could just get a moment alone with his mother.

He took a walk around the verandas of the house so he could look in through the windows of the main buildings to find out where she was, and if she was alone.

As he walked along the West verandah, he saw her in the Drawing Room, embroidering something.

Alone.

So he opened the glass doors and walked in.

"Hello Mother," he bent to kiss her cheek before sitting beside her.

She continued her embroidery, "shall I ring for some tea?"

"There's no need."

"Nonsense," she picked up a small bell from the table beside her and rang it. Almost immediately the newest maid bounded in and, almost as soon was on her way again.

Mrs Fox took up her embroidery again, "now, what's this about son?"

"A young woman broke into my bedroom this morning, and then fell unconscious."

"That's interesting. Where did she come from? And how did she get here?"

"I can't say, though her hair's been cut short, and she's wearing some kind of swimsuit."

"The Yarra Bend Lunatic Asylum I should think," Miss Seagrove said entering the room.

He stood politely, but quickly sat back down, next to his mother, forcing Miss Seagrove to an armchair.

"Perhaps Barnes could make some enquiries," Mrs Fox said, "in the meantime, where will you put her?"

"I'm having the Blue Room made up."

Miss Seagrove hissed, and Mrs Fox and Henry glanced at each other before looking at her.

She shrugged, "I'm not sure the bedroom opposite you is appropriate. Wouldn't it be better to put her in a maid's room at the back of the house?"

Henry for one wasn't having it, "we don't know anything about this woman, she needs to be where I can keep an eye on her."

"That's right Viola," his mother agreed, "Henry can keep us safe if she turns out to be a threat of some kind."

"Mother, I'll need you to arrange some clothing for her, and perhaps someone to take care of her until she wakes up and we know more."

"I can do that," Miss Seagrove said, I want to protect you from walk-in gold diggers."

When Mrs Fox said, "that's a good idea," Henry looked at her aghast, but her face remained inscrutable.

As Miss Seagrove preened, Henry wondered whether his mother was finally feeling the strain of Miss Seagrove's constant presence.

In the meantime, he had little option but to leave the stranger to her "tender" ministrations.

Morag woke suddenly.

She lay awake, eyes closed, trying to figure out what had woken her. Something about Hayward Hall was different.

For one thing, the room smelled as though a female had just exited it, and given she lived alone, that was disconcerting.

To compound matters, she could hear the murmur of conversation, though she couldn't tell how far away it was. Or whether she'd left a television on in the other room.

Additionally, there was something not quite right about the light. In her room, the light and slight breeze from the open window came from her left, and in this room, from the foot of the bed.

She risked opening her eyes.

She was alone.

Looking across a nicer carved bed than her usual one, to a window with a view over a carefully manicured forest instead of over lawn to the stables.

Aside from the bed, there was an old-fashioned matching armoire, chest of drawers and dressing table, as well as a bedside cabinet and chair.

She realised she was in the Blue Room, though the carpet and wallpaper were way more vivid and colourful that in her time.

As you'd expect when you'd travelled 116 years into the past.

She knew there was a toilet behind the stairs, so she struggled out from the covers.

After taking a moment to comprehend, then bunch up the voluminous nightgown someone had put her in, she cautiously opened the door to make sure no one was nearby and scampered down the corridor.

How long had she been out of it?

Long enough for the weather to start warming up.

She washed her hands, bunched up the nightgown and snuck back up the corridor.

Instead of heading around the corner to the room she'd woken up in, she headed across to Henry's room.

She opened the door long enough to check that he was there, but this time, gave herself a moment to fully appreciate how well he looked, here in his element.

Without the strain of hopping from time to time for more than a century, he seemed younger, though she supposed that technically he was.

He might have been wearing the same clothes as the last time she'd seen him, but there was something subtly different about the way this Henry styled his hair to future Henry's styling. He had the same ordinary brown hair and eyes, though the moustache was new to her.

It suited him.

She opened the door fully, and as he looked up to see who was there, she raced across the room to embrace him, "oh Henry, thank goodness you're here. It really worked! You're safe in your own time!"

He tried to disentangle her, "I'm sure I have no idea what you're talking about."

She took a step back to look at him again, trying to pin down what the difference was. "I can't get over how well you look in this time."

She went to embrace him again, but he held her shoulders to stop her from approaching any closer.

"Miss...

"I don't know who you are, or how you know me, or why you feel the need to be so familiar, but I would appreciate it if you would take a step back and explain yourself."

She took a step back, slapped her palm against her forehead, "of course! I forgot you don't know me in this time. I'm Morag Clementine, I'm your future housekeeper, we know each other in the future."

Henry took a few steps back and carefully sat down in a chair, looking at her like she'd escaped from the lunatic asylum.

"Miss Clementine, do you have any idea how ridiculous you sound right now?"

She crossed the room and threw herself on his bed.

He winced.

"Well, I suppose I wouldn't believe me either, but I brought proof. Do you know where my clothes are?"

"Your swimsuit has been laundered and placed in your room, as has some proper clothing. Can you guess what I would prefer you to wear?"

Her swimsuit?

Ah, for some reason she hadn't considered that jungle print leggings and matching tank top might not be the most appropriate clothing to wear.

He ran a finger underneath his collar, and it occurred to her that lying on his bed, naked under her gown, might be doing things to him.

"There's a certain kind of woman who entertains gentleman in bed chambers, and I can only restrain myself so far from taking advantage of the situation.

"Perhaps you could do something about putting some proper clothes on sooner rather than later."

Morag laughed, "I wouldn't have put you down as quite so prim and—"

A young woman threw the door open without so much as a tap at the door, and Henry stood up, "Miss Seagrove, what do you mean by this?"

The woman blushed and took a step back, "I apologise. That woman escaped the bedroom while I was refreshing myself. I assume she made a beeline to your room."

Henry's eyes flicked across to her, and the woman's eyes followed his.

"Oh my goodness, there you are, you little tramp!" She advanced across the room seemingly determined to wrestle her from the bed and out the room.

Morag scrambled backwards on the bed.

"Miss Seagrove," Henry roared.

She stopped and looked over her shoulder at him.

"Can you not see we were having a conversation?"

She drew herself up to her full uptight height, "I do not think it is appropriate for you to interview this woman in her present state of undress. Please allow me to dress her, and continue your conversation somewhere more public, like the Drawing Room, or the Sitting Room."

Morag didn't know what the fuss was about, but when Henry crumpled, it seemed Miss Seagrove had won that round.

He nodded.

Miss Seagrove grabbed her arm with a vice-like grip and dragged her back to the Blue Room.

"You are utterly shameless," Miss Seagrove told her as she helped Morag don a white chemise and drawers.

She handed Morag stockings and cute lace-up boots, frowning as she paced the room while she waited for Morag to get them on.

"Mr Fox is my fiance," she said as she pulled the corset's lacing tighter than Morag thought was necessary, and her heart plummeted.

Henry hadn't mentioned a fiance, and she'd assumed they would pick up where they'd left off.

But, Miss Seagrove was there first, and she could only assume his feelings for the woman were genuine.

She would have to back off.

Miss Seagrove picked up a petticoat, "I would appreciate you keeping your distance." She dragged it over Morag's head, "in fact, the sooner you give up whatever your game is," she held out a flaring frilled navy-blue skirt for Morag to step into, "the better."

She handed Morag a white long-sleeved blouse ruffled on the front and sleeves, then did the buttons on the back up.

Miss Seagrove nodded at her, "and that's how ladies dress, not out in their swimsuits walking the town."

"Oh!"

Morag started opening and closing the drawers looking for the leggings and top.

Or more particularly the locket she'd been wearing when she'd arrived.

"Looking for this?" Miss Seagrove said, letting the necklace dangle from her fingers. "I'm keeping it for now, you can take it back when you leave."

Morag guessed she hadn't opened the locket to see the picture of her and Henry that night in Shanghai. Then again, the locket was a puzzle locket they'd bought there, so it was unlikely she'd be able to open it anyway.

All she had to do, was steal it back.

Miss Seagrove deposited her in the Drawing Room without asking her if she wanted anything to eat.

Rude.

She looked around the cosy room. A piano at one end for night time entertainments, conversational seating with small tables loaded with photos and knickknacks where it would be almost impossible to set your drinks.

Light streamed through the windows and glass doors.

On a day as beautiful as today, she would've opened the doors to let the smell of the rose garden in.

And seeing as no one was there, and she'd been left to her own devices, she walked across the room noting a hidden coffee table holding some embroidery.

She folded the doors open and stepped outside unto the verandah.

Morag was about to take a step down into the garden when a small, well-fed pug arrived.

She bent down to let it sniff her hand, then scratched its head. "You are a darling, aren't you?" she asked it. It didn't reply, though a male voice from above her did, "Dante is indeed a darling."

Henry held out his hand to pull her to her feet, "I see you are now dressed appropriately for your conditions," and he held her hand for longer than was strictly necessary.

Remembering he was someone else's husband to be, she pulled her hand back, held her arms out, and spun around once, "how do you like me now?" she asked.

"Well," he looked her up and down, and she had the feeling that this outfit was sexier than the nightgown she'd worn earlier. "You look fit for decent company at any rate."

Morag smiled ruefully back at him, "I hadn't really thought very much about what would happen when I got here."

Morag's stomach growled, and she rubbed it.

Henry laid a hand on her arm, warm through the thin fabric of her blouse, giving her the jitters. "Have you eaten yet, are you hungry?"

"I am a bit hungry, but I feel like I've been asleep for a week and I need to go for a run."

"Three weeks," he said.

"I'm sorry?"

"You were asleep for three weeks."

"Three weeks?"

Henry smiled as if it were a great joke, and stepped off the verandah. Morag and the dog trailing behind him.

"Yes, we had to get Dr Corrington out to look at you."

"Ffff... I'm so sorry to put you to all that trouble."

She caught up to him, and he tucked her arm through his.

"Nonsense, you've given us all something to talk about."

They took the short route around the Central Lawn and up to the lake.

"So, how did you manage to get inside the house without anyone seeing you?" he asked.

"I told you. I live in the Hall, and I just opened the door. It's the first time I've seen it as your bedroom."

"But if you live in the house in the future, how is this the first time you've seen my bedroom."

Morag paused in the middle of the bridge across the lake, looking out over the water. Dante sat with a small thump.

"I guess seeing as I've fixed it, there's no harm in telling you about it.

"There was some kind of incident on the 9th of September, 1904 that somehow uncoupled you and your room from the rest of the house. So, whenever I opened the door, I never knew when or where you would be."

Henry leaned his back against the railings, looking in the other direction, "it sounds incredible. But you said you had proof?"

"I do, but your fiance took my locket."

Henry stiffened, and Morag hastily backtracked, "I'm sure she's just keeping it safe for me until I leave."

Henry sagged so much Morag turned to support him.

"Well, I believe that solves one of my problems."

"Is there something wrong?"

He smiled, "No Morag, there's nothing for *you* to be concerned about."

Henry set a fast pace back across the bridge, taking the even shorter cut through the pavilion, skirting the pool, and back through the main entrance.

A man met them there, "ah Barnes," Henry said, "would you please ask Mrs Lewis to make up some morning tea and have it brought to the Drawing Room?"

"Yes Sir."

"And do you know where my mother and Miss Seagrove are?"

"I believe your mother is in the Drawing Room Sir, but I'm not sure where Miss Seagrove is."

"Good, make it three for morning tea then. I'll be back with you momentarily."

Mrs Fox was seated on a small sofa embroidering something. She was a small woman, dressed in a relatively simple black dress with a white lace collar and cuffs. She looked up as they entered.

Dante ran to her and sat, leaning on her leg as he slumped to the ground panting.

"Wait here," he said to Morag, then sat next to his mother to hold a whispered conversation. Now and again, she nodded.

Morag feigned an interest in the artwork and vases of flowers.

A young woman arrived with a big tray of sandwiches and cake, followed by an older woman with a large pot of tea, and another with plates, cutlery, cups and saucers.

They deposited them on the now empty coffee table.

Henry beckoned her over, "Mother, may I present Miss Clementine, Miss Clementine, my mother Mrs Fox."

Unsure of the protocol, she sketched a curtsy just in case

Mrs Fox snorted an unladylike snort, "there's no need for that."

She patted the seat beside her, "Henry tells me you haven't had any breakfast, why don't you sit here next to me and eat something."

As Henry left the room, Morag didn't have to be asked twice.

《《 • 》》

Henry smiled grimly; Barnes was still waiting just outside the Drawing Room.

"Come with me," he said, heading towards the stairwell.

On the first floor, he headed to the small dressing room which had been converted to a bedroom to accommodate Miss Seagrove.

He knocked on the door, and there was no answer, so he opened it.

The room was a shambles. He was so sure the prim Miss Seagrove wouldn't condone this kind of mess, he was half convinced there'd been another burglary.

Until he noticed his mother's ivory fan on the dressing table. And his favourite lapis lazuli cuff links. Along with some other trinkets his brothers and sisters had "lost" since the blasted woman had arrived.

For a moment he considered the embarrassment Mr and Mrs Seagrove would face when he sent her back.

But then he thought about how rude she was to the servants and his siblings. Not to mention the things she'd said about Miss Clementine without giving her the chance to defend herself.

And to top it off, that she had dared to threaten them with the things she would do once she was married to him.

It could not be condoned.

"Barnes do you see our missing items there on the dresser?"

"Yes Sir."

"Would you collect it all, and arrange someone to pack Miss Seagrove's belongings."

"Yes Sir."

"Only the things we can be sure she brought with her. Miss Clementine complained Miss Seagrove took her locket, so mind we don't pack anything she hasn't been seen in before."

Barnes nodded and collected the jewellery together, and Henry closed the door behind them.

He watched Barnes head towards the staff quarters, then he went into the Master Suite where he paced up and down swearing violently, thinking that he needed something like a gymnasium to take his feelings out of him.

Instead, he threw his jacket on a chair, went to his bathroom, and splashed cold water on his face.

He sighed and thought some more about Morag.

The hungry way she'd looked at him when she thought he wasn't watching, and the support she'd offered him without knowing he was shocked by Miss Seagrove's misrepresentation of their relationship.

He barely knew Morag, but he liked her. She was easy to be around, not demanding like Miss Seagrove.

He thought she was the kind of person who'd want to read the newspaper in the morning, and imagined bickering amiably with her about that at the breakfast table.

And he remembered their brisk walk about the gardens, how he'd struggled to make her walk at a lady-like pace.

Given the chance, Morag would challenge him and his assumptions every day of his life, but he would enjoy it.

Smiling a little at the thought, he turned to collect his jacket and found Miss Seagrove with a kitchen knife.

Which was a little funny as he hadn't thought that she might even know where the kitchen was.

She advanced into the bathroom, holding it out in front of her, "I won't let her have you," she said, "you belong to me."

Henry held his hands up towards her, "think about what you're saying, Miss Seagrove."

Her face contorted, and she put on a whiny voice to say, "Miss Seagrove, Miss Seagrove." She slashed the knife downwards as she made a noise of frustration, bringing it up again as she asked, "why in God's name won't you call me Viola?"

There wasn't really anything to say to that, so he shrugged, an act that enraged her.

She screamed and lunged towards him, he backed away into the space between the sink and bath, blocking her slash with his forearm and slipping to the ground.

And then screamed again as Miss Clementine slammed her arm into the rim of the bathtub forcing her to drop the knife, and then up behind her back before she could defend herself.

"You right there mate?" she asked as if nothing untoward had happened.

Miss Seagrove was squirming to get away, but Barnes and Roberts had arrived on the scene and carried the kicking and screaming girl away.

"Hey," she called, and the men paused, "send someone back with some bandages okay?" Roberts nodded.

Miss Clementine...

Morag squatted down to his level, "you sure? You look a bit peaky."

She offered him a hand up, but he pulled her down and into a kiss.

Which she returned with the kind of intensity that suggested long term practice.

He was insanely jealous of his future self.

After a time, she pulled away, "you should let me treat that arm."

Reluctantly he held his hand up, and she had no difficulty pulling him up.

Despite himself, he was impressed.

She grabbed a towel, and helped him across to the seat, throwing the towel into his lap as she removed his tie and started unbuttoning his shirt.

He trapped her hand in his, "I'm not sure this is appropriate."

"Don't be ridiculous, you'll bleed to death at this rate. And if you don't, penicillin hasn't been invented yet so you'll die of blood poisoning later."

"Penny what?" he said and dropped his hand, and let her continue.

"Hmmm, not too serious though it looks like you might need stitches. I'll bind it tightly until the doctor can get here." She folded the towel and pressed it against his wound, "hold this tight."

He heard her rummaging around in the bathroom before reappearing with his cologne, "ok, I'm going to pour this on your wound, and it's going to hurt about a billion more times than hell. Okay?"

Almost before she'd finished speaking, she'd started pouring, and it did indeed hurt a billion times more than hell, but he clenched his teeth together and bore it.

Roberts arrived with bandages, "wait," she said to him.

"Ready for more?" she asked Henry folding one of the bandages quickly.

He nodded uncertainly.

She placed the folded bandage on the wound, directed Roberts to hold it, and the arm tightly, then started winding the bandage around his arm to hold it in place. She used her teeth to tear the bandage and tie it around his wrist.

"A couple of pillows please," she said to Roberts and held his arm up above his head until he brought them back. She laid the pillows in his lap and rested his elbow on them, "keep your arm up Henry, it will help stop the bleeding."

"Your blouse," he said looking at the blood.

She grinned, "I don't have to do the laundry while I'm here right?"

Mrs Fox entered the room, "good God," she said when she saw the state of them both. "Did Miss Seagrove cause this?"

Morag made a dismissive noise, "it's nothing."

"We've telephoned for Dr Corrington; he shouldn't be too long He's got a new car and has been itching to try it out.

"Miss Clementine—"

"I think you might call me Morag after this," she waved her hand at Henry.

Mrs Fox inclined her head, "then perhaps you could call me Lily."

"Thank you Lily."

"Morag, perhaps you might like to change your clothes?"

She looked down her body, "I can see that might be the wisest use of my time right now."

She turned to walk away.

"Wait," Henry cried, "what did you come to see me for?"

"What?

"Oh right. Mrs... Lily sent me to see if you were joining us downstairs."

"I expect I might be delayed."

Morag laughed as she left the room.

Of all the things she had seen and done in the last five years with Henry, this had to have been the most exciting. Awake for a day, and she'd saved his life a second time.

Amazing.

And Lily seemed to like her too.

She shimmied out of the blood-stained blue skirt and white blouse, and replaced it with a robe she found in the wardrobe. She went to the bathroom to wash her face, chest and hands.

Back in her room, she donned a russet brown skirt, and a cream, pin-tucked blouse. Then, figuring she should at least put the clothes in to soak, she walked down the back stairs and through to the laundry room.

Of course, it was not the same as her modern house, and she had no idea what to do with all the buckets, mangles, and other equipment she didn't have the names for.

Happily, the young woman with the sandwich tray was on hand to help.

And having been reminded of the sandwiches, she returned to the Drawing Room, and happily for her, the food was still there.

So she helped herself to another sandwich.

And thought about present Henry.

Who wasn't engaged to Miss Seagrove.

And who seemed to like her.

A lot.

He wasn't her Henry, and she felt conflicted about that, but she was quite confident she was stuck in 1904.

With this Henry.

And a Henry in the hand was worth two in the bush.

Dante sat next to her, and she absently fed him a sandwich.

If she couldn't go back to her time, then she would rather be here with a Henry, than out there alone.

If he would have her.

She sat on a sofa in the bay window, looking out into the roses.

And yawned.

Then undid her shoelaces, toed her boots off, and lay down on the sofa. With a scrabble of claws, Dante got up on the couch and snuggled between her legs and the back of the sofa.

《《 • 》》

Henry found them together when he brought Dr Corrington into the Drawing Room to check her over.

Dr Corrington chuckled, and Dante rested his chin on her knees.

"Looks like she's scored another fan," he said scratching Dante's head. "Let's leave her be. By all accounts, she's had an eventful day and probably needs her sleep."

His mother saw the doctor out, while he dropped into a seat and helped himself to a sandwich.

"She's certainly a remarkable woman," he said to his mother as she entered the room.

Mrs Fox sat beside him and stretched her feet out, "if what Dr Corrington said is true, she saved your life."

He pulled the locket he thought was Morag's out of his pocket, and started sliding the pieces around.

"But for what?" he answered, and then told her what Morag'd said about his future.

She thought for a moment, then suggested, "I know she thinks she's averted that future, but you would be wise to look into how you can protect your interests for the future. Open a trust or something."

He didn't want to think about that, but future Henry seemed wise enough to have done something like that.

All of a sudden, the locket fell to pieces in his lap, leaving him holding some small pictures.

He and his mother put their heads together to look at them. The woman was definitely Morag, and the man certainly looked like Henry.

"Shanghai 2216," came a voice behind them, making them jump.

Henry looked up at her, and shuffled to the next picture, "Paris 1925," at the next, "New York 2036," and the next, "The *Destiny* 2765."

Henry flicked through the pictures, looking for something to tell him she was lying.

It still seemed preposterous.

He stood up, dropping the pieces on the floor, "I don't really care where you came from. I just want you to stay. Will you stay?"

Morag snorted, "It's not like men are beating down the door wanting to marry me, and I don't actually have anywhere else to go. Of course I'll stay!"

His mother averted her eyes and helped herself to cake while he kissed Morag within an inch of her life.

THE END

ABOUT THE AUTHOR

Alexandria Blaelock writes stories, some of them for *Ellery Queen's Mystery Magazine* and *Pulphouse Fiction Magazine*. She's also written four self-help books applying business techniques to personal matters like getting dressed, cleaning house, and feeding your friends.

As a recovering Project Manager, she's probably too fond of sticking to plan. She lives in a forest because she enjoys birdsong, the scent of gum leaves and the sun on her face. When not telecommuting to parallel universes from her Melbourne based imagination, she watches K-dramas, talks to animals, and drinks Campari. At the same time.

Discover more at www.alexandriablaelock.com.

BOOKS BY
ALEXANDRIA BLAELOCK

SHORT STORY COLLECTIONS

The Histories of Hayward Hall
Lovelorn, Lovestruck and Love at First Sight
Common or Garden Variety Heroes
Case Files of the Wilkinson Detective Agency
Unavoidable Fates

OTHER FICTION

That Love Nonsense

MS BLAELOCK'S BOOKS

Stress Free Dinner Parties
Signature Wardrobe Planning
Holistic Personal Finance
Minimally Viable Housekeeping
Planning a Life Worth Living

SELECTED SHORT STORIES

Alma's Grace
Balancing the Book
Carmelita Basingstoke
Fate in Your Hands
Kiss of Death
Lady of the Looking Glass
Life in the Security Directorate
Long Weekend in the Snow
Love in the Past Tense
Love in the Security Directorate
Morning Star, Evening Star, Superstar
Needy Bitch
Payton's Run
Phoenix Child
Secret Singer
Shining Star
Ship in a Bottle
Simone Says Hands in the Air
Special Relativity in Space
The Bygone Boyfriend
The Day the Schedule Broke
The Ghost Detectors
The Guardian's Vigil
The Mince Pie Mystery
The Mystery of the Master Suite
The Pseudonym's Bride
The Shadow Thieves
The Time-Space Paradox
Toy Soldiers